Rock Candy
Treasure

Candy Fairies

Rock Candy Treasure

HELEN PERELMAN

ILLUSTRATED BY
ERICA-JANE WATERS

ALADDIN
NEW YORK   LONDON   TORONTO   SYDNEY   NEW DELHI

ALADDIN

An imprint of Simon & Schuster Children's Publishing Division

1230 Avenue of the Americas, New York, New York 10020

First Aladdin paperback edition January 2016

Text copyright © 2016 by Helen Perelman

Illustrations copyright © 2016 by Erica-Jane Waters

Also available in an Aladdin hardcover edition.

All rights reserved, including the right of reproduction in whole or in part in any form.

ALADDIN is a trademark of Simon & Schuster, Inc., and related logo is a registered trademark of Simon & Schuster, Inc.

For information about special discounts for bulk purchases, please contact Simon & Schuster Special Sales at 1-866-506-1949 or business@simonandschuster.com.

The Simon & Schuster Speakers Bureau can bring authors to your live event. For more information or to book an event contact the Simon & Schuster Speakers Bureau at 1-866-248-3049 or visit our website at www.simonspeakers.com.

Cover design by Karina Granda

Interior designed by Tom Daly

The text of this book was set in Baskerville Book.

Manufactured in the United States of America 1215 OFF

2 4 6 8 10 9 7 5 3 1

Library of Congress Control Number 2015955334

ISBN 978-1-4814-4678-5 (hc)

ISBN 978-1-4814-4677-8 (pbk)

ISBN 978-1-4814-4679-2 (eBook)

For Alison Gottsegen

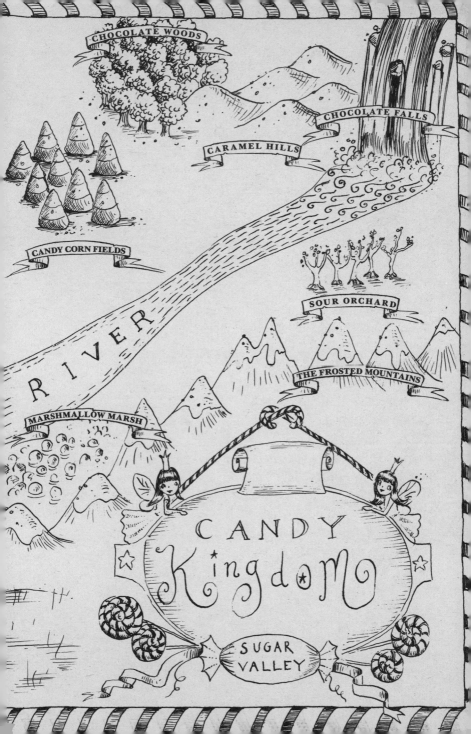

Contents

CHAPTER

1

A New Friend

Melli the Caramel Fairy stood by the hot stones to melt her caramel in a clearing by Caramel Hills. She loved the sounds of Chocolate River rushing down the steep rocks. Chocolate Falls was one of her favorite places in Sugar Valley.

As she watched her pot of melting caramel

dipping sauce, she hummed. She was learning to play a new song on her licorice stick, and she couldn't get the melody out of her head. The song was hard to play, but she wanted to perform it at Candy Castle for Princess Lolli and Prince Scoop. The royal couple was hosting a dinner and had asked some Candy Fairies to play their musical instruments for the entertainment. It was a big honor, and Melli wanted her song to be perfect.

Out of the corner of her eye, Melli saw a bright streak of red and purple. She knew there were no caramel animals with those bright colors.

"Is someone there?" Melli called out. "Hello?"

A branch snapped in the woods, and Melli's heart beat faster.

"Who is hiding in there?" she asked. She had a bad feeling that maybe one of Mogu's Chuchies was hiding in the bushes. Sometimes Mogu the troll would send his little Chuchies to steal candy from Candy Fairies. Or worse than Chuchies, maybe it was Mogu!

Melli wished her other Candy Fairy friends were with her. If Cocoa the Chocolate Fairy were here, she would be brave and strong. Dash the Mint Fairy would be superfast and clever, and Raina the Gummy Fairy would be smart and know a story in the Fairy Code Book that would help. Her friend Berry the Fruit Fairy would likely not be scared at all!

"Hello?" Melli said again. Her voice sounded shaky and unsure.

The leaves on the bush in front of her

moved, and Melli grew more nervous. She tried to think brave thoughts.

"Mogu?" she asked.

"Who's Mogu?" a tiny voice said.

Melli was surprised to hear that reply. Who lived in Sugar Valley and didn't know the greedy, salty troll Mogu, who stole candy and lived in Black Licorice Swamp?

"Who are you?" Melli asked. She fluttered her wings nervously and lifted herself off the ground.

"I'm Crystal," the voice said. "But you can call me Taly. Everybody calls me Taly."

Melli knelt down on the ground where the voice was coming from. Whoever was speaking was small and seemed friendly. Melli peered between the branches. "Hello,

Taly," she said. "I am Melli, a Caramel Candy Fairy."

"Are you a friendly Candy Fairy?" Taly asked.

"Of course!" Melli exclaimed. She saw the tips of tiny, bright candy-apple-red boots.

"I've never seen a Candy Fairy," Taly replied. She stepped from behind the branches and out of hiding.

Melli didn't mean to stare, but she couldn't

take her eyes off the little creature. Taly had a long, pointed head and a red-and-purple striped hat. Her dress was purple with red-and-white polka dots.

"Are you . . . a gnome?" Melli asked.

"Yes, I am. Do you like gnomes?" Taly asked.

Melli laughed. "I've never met a gnome," she said. "My friend Raina once read me a fairy tale about a gnome named Gumbu, but I have never met one."

"I don't know Gumbu," Taly said. She moved closer to Melli and peered behind her back. "Can you fly?" she asked, looking at Melli's wings.

Melli fluttered her wings. "Yes, I can," she said. "See?" She lifted herself up in the air.

Taly's eyes opened very wide. She looked

around at Caramel Hills. "Where am I?"

"This is Caramel Hills," Melli told her. "I live here with other Caramel Fairies."

Taly raised her head and took a big sniff. "What is that smell?" she asked.

"Sweet sugars!" Melli cried. "That is my caramel burning!" She flew over to the hot stones and lifted the pot of bubbling caramel off the hook. "Oh no," she said, peering inside the pot at her burnt caramel.

"Is it ruined?" Taly asked.

Melli stirred the pot. "I think so," she said. She shook her head. "That is not like me at all."

"It's my fault," Taly said. "I'm sorry." The little gnome's eyes filled with tears.

Melli felt terrible that she had made Taly cry. "Don't worry," she said. "There is plenty

more caramel. Would you like something to drink?"

Taly nodded.

"Here," Melli said, giving Taly a cup of fruit nectar. "Drink this, and you can try these caramel squares I made this morning." She reached for her basket of candy on a nearby rock.

"Thank you," Taly said. She ate everything that Melli gave her.

"You haven't eaten in a while, huh?" Melli asked. "Where did you come from, anyway?"

Taly hung her head. "I'm lost," she said quietly. "I'm not supposed to leave the caves, but I needed to find something to fix our carts!"

"Caves?" Melli asked. "Carts?"

Taly pointed to Chocolate Falls. "Rock Candy

Caves," she said. "We use small carts when we mine sugar from the caves."

Melli had no idea what the little gnome was talking about. She had flown around Chocolate Falls many times, and she had never known there were caves . . . with gnomes living there! "You live in caves behind the waterfall?" she asked. "And you mine sugar?"

Taly's small hands flew up to her mouth. "I'm not supposed to tell anyone that!" she said. "Where gnomes live is a secret." She grabbed Melli's hand. "Please promise not to tell anyone."

"Sure as sugar," Melli said. She watched the little gnome eat her treat.

"Will you help me get back home?" Taly asked.

"Fairy's promise," Melli replied quickly. She had to help the little gnome!

As Taly grinned and enjoyed her snack, Melli wondered if would be able to keep the promise she had just made!

Solid Sugar Promise

Melli handed the little gnome another piece of caramel. When she did, she noticed that Taly had started to cry. "If you don't like the caramel, I can get you something else," Melli said quickly. "After all, this is Sugar Valley!"

Taly wiped her eyes with the back of her

hand. "No, I love the caramel," she said. She sniffled. "I'm just not sure how to get home. And I'm scared."

Melli put her arm around the gnome. "I promised to help you," she said, "and I have some very brave and smart friends who can help too."

"But you've never been to Rock Candy Caves," Taly said.

"No," Melli said. She looked toward Chocolate Falls.

Taly licked the caramel off her fingers. "You should come back with me!" She smiled at Melli. "And since we're friends now, I can show you the caves. I am sure that would be okay. If you came with me, then I wouldn't be so scared."

"Why would you be scared?" Melli asked. She was usually the one who was scared and nervous. Looking at the small gnome, Melli suddenly had a burst of confidence. "When I had to go to Ice Cream Isles by myself, I was really scared," she told Taly. "But you know what? I met some really nice friends and I had a great time." She smiled. "I am going to make sure that you get home safely. But we need a little time to make a plan, okay?"

"Okay," Taly said. "Does the plan involve eating more candy?"

"Sure as sugar!" Melli exclaimed.

Taly leaped up and gave Melli a very tight squeeze.

"Friends help each other," Melli said, "and we're friends now."

"Who is your new friend?" a voice cried from above.

The sight of another Candy Fairy sent Taly running. She hid under one of the nearby caramel bushes.

Melli waved to Cocoa. "Come meet Taly," she said. Melli ducked under the branches. "Come out, Taly. Cocoa is my good friend. You are going to love her . . . and her chocolate! She's a Chocolate Fairy!"

Taly stuck her head out of the branches. "A Chocolate Fairy?" she asked.

"At your service!" Cocoa exclaimed as she landed next to Melli. She saw the pointed hat and the little face sticking out of the brushes. "Wait, is that a gnome?" she asked, turning to Melli.

Melli quickly stood up. "Cocoa, this is Taly.

She's a gnome, all right. A lost one." Melli took Taly's hand and brought her out from under the bush. "I promised her that we'd help her get back home."

"We should ask Raina," Cocoa said. She bent down to speak to Taly. "She's our Gummy Fairy friend who will know what to do. She *always* knows what to do."

"Cocoa's right," Melli told Taly. "Raina will check the Fairy Code Book for information about Rock Candy Caves."

"Rock Candy Caves?" Cocoa asked. "I thought that was a made-up place! I think I heard that in a story once."

"It's real," Taly said. She stepped slowly out of hiding. "Gnomes live in secret. I'm not supposed to tell anyone about Rock Candy

Caves. I don't think there will be any real information about gnomes in a fairy book."

"Maybe not," Melli said thoughtfully. "But if anyone can give us information, it would be Raina." She reached out her hand to Taly. "Do you want to take a ride?" Melli fluttered her wings and watched Taly's expression.

"You mean I get to fly?" The little gnome gasped and clapped her hands.

Cocoa laughed. "It's the best way to travel!" she exclaimed. She flew up in the air and did a flip. "Melli can carry you on her back. You are small and light enough."

Taly jumped up and down. "Wow!" she exclaimed. Then she stopped jumping. She bit her fingernails nervously. "I've never flown on a fairy's back before."

Melli smiled at Taly. "No one is ever more nervous than I am! Believe me, you are perfectly safe with me."

Taly climbed up on Melli's back, being very careful of her wings.

"Now hold on tight," Melli said. She lifted off the ground and heard Taly shriek.

"This is so *rocky* cool!" the gnome shouted.

Cocoa looked over at Melli. "What till she meets Dash!" she said, laughing. "She'll have her begging to go flying at a minty speed."

The two fairies flew over Chocolate River to Gummy Forest, where they knew they would find Raina. It was just after lunch, so she was likely feeding the gummy fish in the lake.

Just as Melli had expected, Raina was at the

edge of Gummy Lake with her feeding bucket.

"Berry and Dash are with Raina," Cocoa said. She looked over at Taly. "You're going to get the full five-friend Candy Fairy treatment."

Melli patted Taly's leg as she flew down to Gummy Forest. "I'll take care of this," she said. She landed and helped Taly off her back. Raina, Dash, and Berry turned and saw that Melli and Cocoa were not alone. "I would like you three to meet Taly from Rock Candy Caves," Melli told her friends. "I found her in Caramel Hills."

Dash was the first to fly over. "Hi," she said. "I'm a Mint Fairy. What kind of candy do you make?"

Taly shrugged. "Gnomes don't make candy. We mine the sugar crystals from the caves and send the sugar out into the valley."

"*So mint!*" Dash exclaimed. "So you make the sugar we use to make the candy?"

"We grind up the crystals to make the sugar," Taly explained. "But I've never known what the sugar makes . . . until now!"

Raina and Berry came over and introduced themselves. Melli was proud of how nice her friends were being. Raina even took Taly to see the gummy fish feeding in the lake.

Berry grabbed Melli's arm. "Are you in sugar shock?" she whispered into Melli's ear. "Fairies and gnomes are not known for getting along. Don't you remember the fairy tales we used to read about gnomes?"

"What do you mean?" Melli asked. "Taly has been so gentle and sweet. She's lost, Berry. I *promised* I would help her. And you know those stories weren't all true."

"I guess the gnome part was true," Raina added.

"What about the bigger gnomes she lives with?" Berry asked Melli. "What if they are not as friendly to Candy Fairies?"

Melli watched Raina and Taly over by Gummy Lake. What was Berry getting so upset about? Taly was a lost gnome who needed their help. Plus, Melli had made a promise. This was not how she had imagined the meeting with her friends would go.

CHAPTER

3

Sweet Discoveries

Taly pulled on Melli's arm. "Your friend Raina showed me how to feed the gummy fish," she said. "There were so many of them! And so many bright colors!"

Melli smiled. "Taly, I'm sure you were a great help," she said.

"I had no idea that this Gummy Forest

exists!" Taly exclaimed. "Candy Kingdom is beautiful!"

"Now you've got her hooked on gummy fish and Candy Kingdom," Berry whispered to Melli. "This is going to get very sticky."

Melli glared at Berry. Why was she being so unhelpful? "She's just exploring and learning about a new place," Melli told Berry.

"Is everything all right?" Dash asked. She looked between Melli and Berry. She could tell that the two friends were disagreeing about something. Dash flew over and took Taly's hand. "Come with Cocoa and me to meet Blue Belle the gummy bear," she said.

A smile spread across Taly's face. Melli loved seeing Taly so happy.

"I'll be right back," Taly called over her shoulder.

Melli waved as Dash and Cocoa took Taly off to meet Blue Belle. "Thanks, Dash," she called.

"We need to talk," Raina said, flying over to Melli.

Melli shook her head. "Oh no," she replied. "Are you going to be like Berry?"

"Berry is right to be worried," Raina said. "It's not every day that fairies and gnomes hang out together. In fact, I don't know if they ever have!"

"You sound like Berry," Melli said, a bit more angrily than she meant to. "Maybe we should start hanging out with the gnomes."

"Don't get upset, Melli," Berry said. "We're just a little concerned."

"I thought you'd help," Melli said. "Or at least I thought you'd *want* to help. Taly is lost.

She was really afraid. If I were lost, I would hope someone would offer to help me."

Raina and Berry looked at each other, and Melli could tell they both felt bad.

"You're right," Raina told her. "We need to get Taly home. Let's do some research. You can't go flying into a gnome's cave without a plan."

Melli felt better knowing that her friends were going to help. She knew very little about gnomes and caves. "Do you have a book about gnomes, Raina? Remember that story about Gumbu? She was a gnome."

Raina scratched her head. "Gumbu's a fairy tale," she said. "Maybe there is a Lupa story."

All the Candy Fairies loved Lupa stories. The brave Candy Fairy Lupa had had many adventures and had written exciting books about her experiences.

Berry looped her arm around Melli. "Let's all go to Raina's library to look while Dash and Cocoa are with Taly. I'll bet we can find some bit of information."

The three fairies flew to check out Raina's bookshelves. It always amazed Melli to see all of Raina's books lined up so neatly. Raina was one of the most organized Candy Fairies. She had to be—she had more books than any other fairy in the kingdom and Princess Lolli had trusted her with the treasured Fairy Code Book.

"Ah, let's try this one," Raina said, pulling a thin book off the top shelf. "I think there is a chapter or two in this book about gnomes."

As Raina flipped through the pages, Melli took down a book of Lupa stories. Lupa had so many adventures, it was hard to find the one about gnomes!

"You might want to check the blue Lupa book over on that shelf," Raina said.

Melli flew up to get the blue book. She had no luck. Then she spotted a green-apple-candy-colored book, *Sugar Tales*. Melli opened the book and saw one chapter that made her heart leap. "Sweet discoveries!" she exclaimed. "The chapter is called 'Gnomes in Caves,'" On the first page of the chapter, Melli saw a fairy wearing a warm jacket and a light strapped around her head. "Look at this," Melli said. She turned the book around so Berry and Raina could see.

"Lickin' lollipops," Berry said. "I think you've just discovered the outfit you need to go exploring in the caves." She leaned over Melli's shoulder. "I could let you borrow my cotton candy and fruit leather jacket. And I'm sure Dash could figure out how to make a peppermint headlight for you."

Melli loved how Berry was now trying to help. Berry loved fashion, and of course she had just the right outfit for Melli to wear on a cave adventure. "Thank you, Berry," she said. "It looks like it is pretty dark and cold in the caves."

Raina turned around the book she was reading. She pointed to a drawing of a gnome's cave that was full of twists and turns. "We need to come up with a way for you to find your way out of there," she said. "It's like a maze. You'd have to track your way in to find the way out!"

Berry snapped her fingers. "I know what to do!" she exclaimed. "We can weave you a licorice rope, and that way you can follow the licorice out of the caves once Taly is home."

Melli reached over to hug her friends. "You both are the best," she said. "Thanks for helping figure this plan out. I can't wait to tell

Taly that we have a way to get her back home!"

"We hope," Raina added.

Trying not to take Raina's comment the wrong way, Melli raced out to find Taly. She felt sure that this plan was going to work and Taly would get home safely.

CHAPTER 4

Licorice Loops

Back in Caramel Hills, Taly listened to Melli practice her licorice stick. Now that a plan was set to return to the caves later in the day, there was some time to rest and for Melli to practice for her performance.

"That was *rocking* sweet!" Taly exclaimed. "Melli, you are so good on the licorice stick.

I wish I could see you play at Candy Castle."
Taly leaned back on a caramel oak tree. "I bet
that castle is amazing."

"Candy Castle is *sugar-tastic*," Melli said.
"And Princess Lolli and Prince Scoop are the
sweetest, but I've just learned this song, so I'm
a little nervous."

Taly stood up. "You are very good," she said.

Melli put her instrument back in the case.
"Thank you," she said, blushing. "The party
is tomorrow. I wish I had a little more time to
practice."

"You'll be great," Taly said, smiling.

"Berry, Raina, Dash, and Cocoa will be here
any minute," Melli said. "They are getting the
supplies. The plan is to get to the caves before
Sun Dip."

"Sun Dip?" Taly asked. "What is that?"

"When the sun dips down and night begins," Melli told her. She pointed out the window and up to the Frosted Mountains. "When the sun dips below the mountaintops, the whole sky turns delicious colors. It is my favorite time of day."

Taly gazed up at the iced mountaintop. "I've never seen a Sun Dip before," she said. "Inside the caves we don't get to the see the sky."

Melli sat down next to Taly. "Why do gnomes stay in their caves and never come out?"

"I'm not sure," Taly replied. "That is part of the reason I wanted to go outside the caves. But then I got lost—and scared."

"Did you tell anyone you were leaving to explore?" Melli asked. She had not asked Taly before about her reasons for leaving. She wanted to be careful not to upset her or make her feel uncomfortable.

Taly looked down at the ground. "No," she said. "And I bet Mama G will be angry. She says I do things without thinking sometimes."

"We say that about Dash sometimes too," Melli said. "I'll bet Mama G is very worried."

Taly's eyes filled with tears. "I didn't mean to worry her," she said. "I was just so curious about what was outside the caves. Most gnomes don't think about that sort of thing."

"There is nothing wrong with being curious," Melli said. "But maybe next time you should let someone know what you are up to." She gave the little gnome a hug. It felt good to be the one calming someone else. For the first time, Melli wasn't nervous or scared. She was feeling hopeful and knew that her friends would come through with their plan to get Taly back to her caves safely.

"Have ever seen a sugar crystal from Rock Candy Caves?" Taly asked.

Melli thought for a moment and shook her head. "What does it look like?"

"Sugar crystals grow in our caves," Taly explained. "They hang from the ceilings and create *sugar-tastic* shapes and sometimes colors."

"Will you show me some when we go to the caves later?" Melli asked.

"You bet!" Taly said. She smiled up at Melli. "And thank you for being so nice to me. You and your friends are the nicest fairies any gnome could hope to meet."

Melli laughed and gave Taly a tight squeeze. "Sure as sugar! Anytime!" she said. "Now come on, it's time to meet the others at Chocolate Falls."

Taly jumped up onto Melli's back and together they flew over to Chocolate Falls. Melli hoped they would be able to find the cave opening easily.

The other Candy Fairies were there—even Berry! Melli was touched that Berry was on time. The fashion-minded fairy was always fashionably late!

"Come try on your mining outfit," Berry called when she saw Melli and Taly.

Slipping on the warm jacket and then the headlight, Melli felt like a real adventurer.

"You look like Lupa!" Cocoa cried.

"I hope I can be as brave as Lupa," Melli whispered to her friend. "Especially since I'll be on my own with Taly."

Berry pulled out the long licorice rope. "Don't worry," she said. "We will be on the other end of this rope, ready to come get you."

Melli was so thankful for her friends. "Taly, this plan is going to work," she said. "You'll see. We'll have you back in no time."

Raina and Berry uncoiled the licorice rope and stood back from the cave opening.

"We'll be right here," Raina said. She looped one end of the licorice around Melli's belt.

"Be careful," Cocoa told Melli.

"And bring back some treats!" Dash exclaimed. She blushed when her friends turned to look at her. "Taly and I were talking about some gnome sweet treats, and they sounded minty good!"

Taly laughed along with the other Candy Fairies. Melli was happy that Dash had cracked a joke. She gave her a hug. "I will be sure to bring you back a treat," she said.

"You know the way once you are inside, right?" Raina asked Taly. "You will lead Melli. The rope is for Melli to find her way back out."

"Got it," Taly said. "I really liked meeting you all. I hope maybe we can see one another again."

"Me too," Berry said.

Melli was so proud of Berry.

"Off we go," Melli said, taking Taly by the hand.

Melli looked back at her friends, gripping the rope. It was a safe feeling, seeing her friends standing there holding the anchor. Especially since she had no idea where she and Taly were going! Where was this gnome home entrance?

"I think it is this way," Taly said to Melli. "It's dark, but gnomes can see in the dark. Follow me." She tightened her hand around Melli's. "I'm glad you are here with me."

"Me too," Melli said. She walked behind Taly and noticed that the tunnels curved and twisted just like in the story she had read. She was glad that she had Berry's warm coat. It was very cold in the caves.

"We are close, I think," Taly said. She stopped. She turned. "Or maybe we should go this way?" Taly took her striped hat off and scratched her head.

The tunnels were dark and twisty. No wonder Taly had gotten lost!

Melli looked up, and her headlamp put a spotlight on a sugar crystal hanging down from the ceiling. "Whoa, what is that?" she asked.

"That is a sugar crystal," Taly said proudly. "And now I know where we are! Come this way!" She pulled Melli away from the large crystal and around a bend.

Melli held her breath. "Oh, sweet sugars," she said. "Taly, that is just amazing!" Hanging down were clusters of colorful crystals in a

rainbow of colors. She moved closer to view the crystals.

"This all looks familiar now," Taly said. "Come!"

There were a few more twists and turns. And then Melli realized something . . . The licorice loop around her belt was no longer there! She was not attached to her friends.

"Hot caramel!" Melli cried. "The licorice rope broke!"

CHAPTER 5

Home Sweet Home

Melli's heart began to beat a thousand times faster than normal. Her face felt a hot cinnamon color. Now that the rope had broken, she was sure she'd never find her way out! She looked behind her and didn't see the licorice rope. "Oh no," she wailed. "I have no idea where the rope fell off."

"I'm sure Mama G will be able to help," Taly said. "She is our leader and very smart. She might be upset with me, but I am sure she will be kind to you. Especially after all the help you and your friends have given me."

Somehow Melli had not focused on meeting Mama G and the other gnomes until right at that minute. "How does Mama G feel about Candy Fairies?" Melli asked.

Taly shrugged innocently. "I don't really know. She never talks about Candy Fairies or anything outside the gnome world. I didn't even know what a Candy Fairy was until I met you! I never really thought about what happened to the sugar after the carts left the caves."

This news didn't make Melli feel any better.

"What happens if she doesn't trust or like Candy Fairies?" Melli asked. She thought of Berry's reaction when she first met Taly. What would happen if this Mama G gnome felt the same way about Candy Fairies?

Melli's wings were fluttering and her feet lifted off the ground.

"Hold on," Taly said. "I know that's my sugar rock!" She pulled Melli forward. The tiny gnome dragged Melli along a narrow tunnel and then around a few large sugar crystals. With each step Melli grew more concerned that she was getting farther away from her licorice rope—and the exit.

"Is this home?" Melli asked when they arrived in a clearing. Up ahead Melli could see a group of gnomes of all shapes and sizes.

They wore colorful pointed hats and were standing around a map hanging on the cave wall. Melli could hardly believe her eyes, there were so many gnomes here!

"Crystal!" one of the larger gnomes cried. The larger gnome rushed toward Taly and swept her up in a tight, long squeeze.

Melli tried to think what brave Lupa the explorer would do in this situation. Melli was possibly the first Candy Fairy these gnomes had ever seen. She gathered her courage and smiled as wide as she could. "Hello," she said, "I am Melli the Caramel Candy Fairy, and I have brought Crystal back home."

A silence fell over the gnomes. None of them spoke. They all looked at Melli in disbelief. Melli heard the quiet drops of sugar water trickling through the caves. She tried not to panic, but this silent greeting was making her wings twitch.

Finally, the tallest gnome, with a green hat, stepped forward. Melli could hear the crunch of the pebbles on the ground as she walked toward her. She couldn't tell if the gnome was happy or angry. As she got closer Melli saw that she was smiling.

"I am Mama G," the gnome said. "Thank you for bringing Crystal home. We were very worried about her."

Melli bowed her head. She curtsied as if she were in front of the king and queen. "It is an honor to meet you," Melli said. "I have heard stories of a brave gnome named Gumbu. Is that you?"

"Gumbu was my grandmother," Mama G said. "She was a brave explorer."

Melli couldn't wait to tell Raina and Berry that the Gumbu stories were real!

"I really enjoyed getting to know Taly," Melli told Mama G. "She has told me so many interesting things about gnomes."

"I see," Mama G said. She looked over at Taly. "She is our little adventurer. But she needs to think before she acts." Mama G turned to Taly. "We were so worried. We didn't know what happened to you. You are so lucky to have met a nice Candy Fairy."

Taly lowered her head. "I know I was wrong," she said. "But you all were wrong about outside the caves. Sugar Valley is beautiful and full of delicious candy and very nice Candy Fairies."

Melli smiled at Taly. Then she noticed the other gnomes were whispering and gesturing, and Melli wasn't sure what was happening. Were they angry at Taly? Were they afraid of Melli?

Just at that moment a loud siren sounded.

The noise echoed throughout the tunnel. The gnomes scattered and hid behind rocks and inside hidden passageways.

"What is happening?" Melli asked Taly. She was being pushed and shoved to the side as the gnomes took to their hiding places.

"It's a warning alarm," Taly told her quickly. "There are some passages that have signals to warn us of danger. Come, there is no time to waste. You must come hide with Mama G and me."

Taly held out her hand, and Melli, taking it, followed her to a small opening off to the side of the clearing. Suddenly the area was clear of gnomes, and all she could hear was the wailing alarm. When the siren stopped, there was silence.

"We need to wait until we get the all-clear signal," Taly said.

"Does this happen often?" Melli asked.

"No," Taly said. "We've had practices, but I've never actually heard the siren go off for real."

This made Melli feel even more afraid. Who knew what or who was in the caves with them!

CHAPTER 6

Surprises

Taly stuck her head up over the rock and reported back to Mama G and Melli. "I don't see a thing," she said. "Mama G, could it be a false alarm?"

"I don't believe so," Mama G said. She stared at Melli and her fluttering wings.

Melli stood with her back against the wall.

She was feeling very aware that she was the only one in the caves with wings.

"Wait!" Taly cried. "I do see something." She scooted out of the opening.

"No!" Mama G scolded. She lunged for her little gnome, pulling her back into the dark. "Don't put yourself in harm's way, Crystal. Stand back." She gave Taly a long, cold look. "Remember, you must *think* before you *act*," she said.

Melli moved toward Taly. "Let me look," she said as bravely as she could. She switched places with Taly. She knew that Taly was trying to be helpful, but Mama G was right. Taly hadn't really thought before she wandered out into Caramel Hills. And now she really shouldn't be the lookout.

Down the dark tunnel, Melli could make out some figures. The shadows on the wall made it hard to see. All at once Melli clapped her hands and burst into a happy shriek. "It's my friends!" she called.

Raina, Berry, Cocoa, and Dash flew down the tunnel to Melli. There was lots of hugging. Dash was holding a large peppermint light that cast large shadows all around them.

"We were so worried when the licorice rope broke," Cocoa said. "We pulled the rope, and when we saw the end of it, we had to come and find you."

"We were careful to mark our way in with mint crème that glows in the dark," Dash said proudly.

Melli spun around. "Please come out of hiding," she called. "Come meet my friends. We are Candy Fairies, and we live outside these caves in Sugar Valley. We would all like to be your friends. I know you have the alarm to warn you against unwanted guests, but these fairies are friendly—fairy promise!"

"Mama G," Taly said, looking up at her mother, "these are the fairies who were so nice to me and brought me back here."

A smile spread across the large gnome's face. "If these fairies showed you kindness," she said, "we should show them every bit of kindness as well."

Slowly, the many gnomes came out of hiding. They stepped slowly toward the five fairies.

"Welcome to Rock Candy Caves," Mama G said.

"Thank you," Melli said. "It is an honor to meet you all and to see your beautiful home."

Mama G looked pleased. "You are the first fairies we've ever had here. Not many fairies would come into these caves like this. You must be brave and loyal friends. Please follow me. We will get you some warmer clothes. Our caves are too cold for fairies without proper hats and coats."

Taly smiled. "She likes you! She likes you!" she chanted.

Everyone laughed. Taly's happiness was so nice to see. Melli was pleased the reunion was going so well. And she was excited to have her friends with her. After the Candy Fairies got extra coats and gnome hats, Mama G showed them around. There were sugar crystals hanging from the ceiling and so many bright neon colors. Carved into the rock walls were doors that led to where the gnomes lived. Each door had different carvings and looked as if someone had spent a lot of time working to make the doors perfect. Never would Melli have imagined that the inside of a gnome cave would be so bright and beautiful. Melli would not have been able to describe all the sights and sounds of the caves to her friends. She was so glad they were able to see the colors of the rock candy crystals with her.

"Sweet strawberries!" Berry said. "This must have taken you forever to build."

"Well, gnomes have lived here for many, many

years," Mama G said. "Gnomes lived in the caves longer than fairy queens and kings in Sugar Valley." She stopped in front of a wall covered with drawings of gnomes. "Here you can see the story of the first gnomes in the area."

Raina flew up closer to the drawings. With a peppermint in her hand, she looked closely at the drawings from long ago. "*Sweet sugars!*" she said. "I don't remember ever seeing any of these kinds of paintings in any books. I never knew that gnomes had such a long history in Sugar Valley. Candy Fairies *should* know about this."

"It is good for us to learn about each other," Mama G told them.

"Thank you for showing us these," Melli said. "We are so honored. And we have really liked getting to know Taly. Running off like she did was wrong, but we are so glad that we had the chance to meet her and to learn about the gnomes."

"Show them the special crystals," Taly said, jumping up and down. "Wait till you see these," she said to the Candy Fairies.

Mama G patted Taly on the head. "You can show your friends the treasures," she said.

The Candy Fairies followed Taly down another long, twisting tunnel until the space opened up again to show hundreds of rock candy crystals. Some were growing from the ground up and some were hanging down from the ceiling. These colorful crystals were delicious and brighter than the others.

"*Sugar-tastic!*" Melli exclaimed. "Now I know

why you call them treasures. I have never seen anything like these."

The Candy Fairies were in awe at the sight of the colors, shapes, and sizes of the precious rock candy.

"These are so different from the candy on Rock Candy Isle," Cocoa said.

Mama G's large ears perked up. "I have only heard about that isle in the Vanilla Sea from books. Is it really beautiful?"

"Yes," Melli said. "It is small, but the candy from there is very sweet."

"You should let Princess Lolli know about all these treasures," Cocoa told her.

"Who is Princess Lolli?" the gnome asked.

Melli quickly realized that these gnomes knew nothing about the world outside the caves. "Princess Lolli is the ruling fairy princess of Sugar Valley. Her parents are Queen Sweetie and King Crunch."

"There is a dinner at the castle tomorrow," Cocoa said.

"Yes!" Melli said excitedly. "Would you and Taly consider coming as our guests?"

"Melli is going to be playing her licorice stick," Taly said. "Please, Mama G?" she begged. "I'd love to go to Candy Castle!"

Mama G looked nervous. "I'm not sure I am up for such a trip," she said. "I will think about it."

Dash flew over to a row of carts that were beat-up and each missing a wheel or two. "What are these?" she asked.

"These are the carts we fill with sugar," Taly

told her. "We mine the sugar from the caves and send the carts out to Sugar Valley."

"And before this you never left the caves?" Berry asked.

"No," Taly said. "But I always wondered where the sugar went."

Melli looked over at Dash. She saw her friend's face as she looked at the broken cart she knew the Mint Fairy was thinking fast.

"Dash, do you have an idea about how to fix these carts?" Melli asked.

Dash grinned. "Sure as sugar! These carts are similar to sleds, except there are wheels, not blades, on the bottom," she said, giggling. "I think this will be an easy fix."

"That might be just the thing to get Mama G to seriously consider our Candy Castle invitation! She would see how we want to be friends and help out." She hoped Dash would be able to fix the run-down carts.

7

Sweet Fixings

What do you think, Dash?" Melli asked. She watched Dash examine the carts.

The handy fix-it Mint Fairy was trying to see what needed to be done. Dash held up a hand to signal she needed more time.

"If Dash fixes the carts," Melli whispered to Cocoa, "the gnomes would sure warm up to us." She looked over at Mama G and the other gnomes, who were staring at the five Candy Fairies.

"I don't think they know what to do about us," Cocoa said.

Melli stepped forward. "My friend Dash can help fix your carts," she said.

There was complete silence.

"We definitely surprised them," Raina whispered. "Think about it. These gnomes have never seen anyone different from themselves. They're scared."

Melli realized how strange it was for the gnomes to have Candy Fairies in their caves, but it was strange to be a Candy Fairy in a gnome's cave too!

"I need to get this wheel off," Dash said.

"Do you think you can hold the cart up while I take the wheel off?" she asked.

"We can help," Mama G said. She waved her hand for another gnome to come over. It was easy for the two gnomes to lift the cart up high enough for Dash to slip off the broken wheel.

"Thank you," Dash said.

"Was that wheel the problem?" Mama G asked.

The wheel was bent out of shape. It was no wonder the cart wasn't moving so well.

"The bent wheel is part of the problem," Dash said, "but there are some other repairs that should be made for the cart to run smoothly."

"That doesn't look good," Taly added, peering up at the bent wheel.

"Actually, the wheel isn't so bad," Dash told Taly. "I have to straighten this piece," she said, pointing to the bent spoke. "All the carts seem to have bent wheels. I can fix that." She reached over to her bag and pulled out some tools.

"You have your tools with you?" Melli asked in amazement.

"Sure as sugar!" Dash replied. "I never leave home without tools."

Dash set to work on the broken wheel. Cocoa

and Raina were at her side, and Melli knew they'd get the broken carts working again.

"These carts will be good as new in no time," Berry said.

Mama G shook her head in disbelief. "Can you really fix them?"

"Friends help one another," Melli said. She winked at Taly.

"Mama G," Berry said boldly, "I think there are many Candy Fairies who would love to see these candy crystals. This is a natural wonder!"

Mama G looked confused. "Gnomes have never gone outside our tunnels. I don't think these crystal forms have ever been used for anything except to make more sugar. We never thought anyone else would appreciate their beauty."

Melli moved forward. "Oh, that isn't true at all," she said. "Candy Fairies would love and appreciate these crystals."

"Perhaps we can try to make something," Berry said. "We could make scrumptious treats or even a beautiful tiara."

"Gnomes don't usually stray from caves," Mama G said, looking down at Taly. "Except my curious adventurer." She hugged her little gnome. "If only she had told me where she was going!"

"You never would have let me go!" Taly said, laughing.

"That is true," Mama G said. "But at least I would have known where to look for you! Do you know how many tunnels are here in Rock Candy Caves?"

Taly hung her head. "A lot," she said.

"I don't blame Taly for being so curious," Mama G told Melli. "I just want her to think before she steps."

"Especially if she is stepping outside the caves," Melli said.

Mama G laughed. "Exactly."

Melli liked Mama G, and suddenly she felt more comfortable. "Please think about coming to the dinner at Candy Castle," she said. "Princess Lolli and Prince Scoop are very generous and kind. You'll love meeting them. And I know they would want to know about these scrumptious rock candy crystals."

"I am not sure," Mama G said. "We are not like Candy Fairies."

"Mama G, please can we go?" Taly asked.

Mama G shifted her weight back and forth on her large, wide feet. Melli could tell this was a hard decision for the gnome.

"Please come," Melli said. "We promise to stay with you the whole time."

"You'll love the royal dinner," Dash said, perking up. "Best candy in the whole kingdom—fairy promise!"

No one said a word. All the gnomes were waiting to hear what Mama G would say.

"Please, Mama?" Taly said.

Melli wasn't sure what the gnome was going to say. She hoped the answer would be yes.

"If you promise to stay near me the whole time," Mama G said to Taly. "No running off."

Taly agreed quickly. Mama G looked at the Candy Fairies. "This will be an important

meeting. Candy Fairies and gnomes together—who would have ever thought that was possible!"

Melli grinned. "It's a delicious thought, and I'm looking forward to it."

Taly jumped up and down. "I get to go to Candy Castle!" she cheered. She ran over to Melli. "And now I get to see you play your licorice stick. It is going to be a super *rocking* night!"

"In the meantime," Mama G said, "please stay the night here. You are our welcomed guests. It is late, and we all could use a good night's rest before our big Candy Castle day."

"Thank you," Melli said. She couldn't wait for tomorrow to come!

Wheels and Worries

First thing the next morning, Dash started to rebuild the carts, along with a few gnomes eager to learn how to fix them. Melli was amazed at how quickly Dash was able to work. Taly was a great assistant, and it seemed as if those old carts were going to work better than before.

"Remember," Melli said to Dash, "these carts don't have to go as fast as your sleds!"

Dash was one of the fastest Candy Fairies in Sugar Valley. She had won lots of trophies for her fast sledding and knew a great deal about building and fixing sleds.

Dash chuckled. "I know," she said. "Sleds are similar but different." She held up one of the bent wheels from the cart. "Sleds don't have wheels, and that is the tricky part!"

Berry, Raina, and Melli began work on a special dress for Mama G's castle visit while the others worked on the carts. There was so much to get done!

Seeing her friends and Taly work together made Melli feel deliciously happy. Not only had they gotten Taly home safely, but also they were helping the gnomes.

"This is quite a sight," Raina said, coming up beside her. She put her arm around Melli. "Gnomes and fairies working together. Princess Lolli and Prince Scoop are going to love this!"

"I hope so," Melli said softly. "I am getting

a little nervous about introducing the gnomes at the castle dinner. I hope everyone there will be welcoming."

"Why wouldn't they be? The gnomes are peaceful and kind," Raina said.

"But also a big surprise," Melli added. "You didn't know about the gnomes living in Rock Candy Caves. I am sure most Candy Fairies don't either."

"That doesn't mean they shouldn't know or they won't be kind," Raina told her. "You worry too much, Melli."

Melli fluttered her wings nervously. "Yes, I know," she said. "But even Berry was unsure about meeting the gnomes in the beginning."

Raina shook her head. "Don't worry, Melli. It is going to be a supersweet night!"

Just then Melli heard Dash yell.

"No, Taly!" Dash hollered.

Melli looked back and saw Taly jump into the cart and rush past her friends on a steep hill heading deeper into the caves. Dash was holding the steering wheel in her hand.

"There's no steering in that cart!" Dash yelled after her.

Melli flew down the tunnel as fast as she could. She was closer than Dash to the track and had a head start. Even so, she wasn't sure she could reach the cart in time. Without a steering wheel, the cart could slam into the stone wall.

Melli's wings were aching, but she had to reach the cart. "Hold on, Taly!" she cried.

"I can't stop!" Taly screamed. She looked

back at Melli. Her purple-and-red hat was flopping in front of her eyes as she gripped the side of the cart.

"I can almost reach you," Melli called. She stretched out her hands as far as she could. With her last bit of energy, Melli got close enough to the cart to grab Taly's elbow. She lifted Taly up just as the cart crashed into the side of the tunnel.

"Are you all right?" Melli asked. She gently laid Taly down on the side of the track. Melli was panting so hard, she could barely speak.

Taly nodded. Her eyes were stuck on the damaged cart. "You saved me," she said. "Thank you, Melli. I am so sorry." The little gnome hung her head. "I always seem to be sorry."

The other Candy Fairies flew over to them.

They were so relieved to see that Taly was not hurt.

"Taly, you need to think before you run off to do something," Cocoa told her. "What were you trying to do, anyway?"

"I thought I would take the cart for a test run," she said.

"I know I like to do things fast too. But you need to be safe," Dash added.

"I am sorry," Taly said.

"Acting fast is not always the best," Dash told her. "Especially when you don't think about what will happen next."

"Like exploring outside Rock Candy Caves without telling anyone, or taking a cart before it is tested," Taly said.

Melli sighed. "Exactly."

"I promise to be more careful," Taly said. "I promise. Especially when we're at Candy Castle."

"You don't need to promise that," Mama G said. She waddled over to the circle of fairies. "You are not going to Candy Castle. Not after the stunt you've pulled here today."

The five Candy Fairies weren't sure what to say. And Melli had a feeling that Mama G wasn't going to change her mind. Would the meeting of the Candy Fairies and gnomes ever happen?

CHAPTER
9

Sharing Treasures

You have proven that you cannot listen, and I don't want to risk us all getting into trouble." Mama G stomped her large foot and turned to walk away.

Melli looked over at Taly. The little gnome's eyes were red, and her upper lip was trembling. "Oh, Taly," she said. "I am so sorry."

"I have to change her mind," Taly said, sniffing. "I really want to go to Candy Castle. I wanted to see you play, and to meet Princess Lolli and Prince Scoop. I wanted Mama G to see Sugar Valley. I just have to convince her!"

Melli glanced at her friends. They all looked down at the ground. It was hard to ignore the anger and certainty in Mama G's voice. Taly had broken a rule. Again. And broken Mama G's trust.

"Mama G is really angry, Taly," Melli whispered. "What you did was very wrong."

"She has to change her mind," Taly said, wiping her nose with the back of her hand. "This is too important." She looked up at the Candy Fairies. "I know what I did was wrong."

"Anyone have any ideas?" Melli said, turning to her friends.

"She really doesn't seem like the type of gnome to change her mind," Cocoa said.

"I don't blame her," Dash mumbled. She looked down at the bashed-up cart.

Melli gave Dash a stern look. "We have come so far," she pleaded. "I know I was nervous about the gnomes coming to the castle dinner, but think of how exciting it would be, for the gnomes and all the Candy Fairies to meet."

"You're right," Dash said. "But what can we do? What Taly did was wrong." She bent down to look at the damage to the cart. "This cart was almost fixed, and now it's a mess."

"Maybe you can talk to Mama G," Taly said.

"You can get her to see that I am very sorry."

Melli smiled and looked directly at the little gnome. "Someone needs to talk to Mama G," she said. "But it *isn't* a Candy Fairy."

Taly slowly nodded. "I had a feeling you were going to say that," she said. "I just don't know what to say to change her mind."

"You have to prove to her that you are serious about keeping your word and paying attention to rules," Melli told her. "Especially when you are at Candy Castle."

"How am I going to do that?" Taly asked. She sat down on a rock candy with a thump. She put her chin in her hand and pouted.

"Be honest with her," Melli said.

"Princess Lolli always tells us that honesty will get you far," Raina added.

Dash put her arm around Taly. "I've been in stickier situations," she said. "You can do this. Maybe you could think of a punishment for yourself."

"That's a great idea," Berry said.

Taly stopped looking so sad and suddenly looked up at her new friends. "I can clean up the mess I made here," she said. She jumped up and started to clear out the broken pieces of cart.

The five Candy Fairies wanted to help, but they knew this was a job that Taly had to do by herself. The little gnome was serious about her work and cleaned up the pieces. And Melli noticed that the Candy Fairies weren't the only ones who were watching. She spotted Mama G hiding behind a rock, watching Taly.

When the broken pieces of the cart were neatly in a pile, Mama G came out from behind the rock. She went over to Taly and pulled her aside. "Never have I seen you clean up after you made a mess," she said. "I can see how sorry you are. These new friends of yours must really be helping you."

"Sure as sugar!" Taly cried. She glanced over at the Candy Fairies, who were trying to look as if they were not listening. "Can we please go to Candy Castle?" she asked. "I promise I will listen and behave."

Mama G paused for a moment. She watched Taly and then glanced over at the Candy Fairies. "I believe you," she said. "And I think it would be our honor to go meet the princess and prince and present them with sugar crystals from Rock Candy Caves."

The Candy Fairies all cheered. Melli swooped over to Taly.

"And," Mama G said, putting her large hand up, "there will be no rock exploring or playing in the tunnels for a week."

Taly hung her head. "I understand," she said.

"I am proud of you," Mama G continued. "I am glad you are taking responsibility for what you've done." She turned to Melli. "You have been such a good friend to Taly. Thank you."

"I'm so happy that you and Mama G will come tonight!" Melli exclaimed. "This is going to be the sweetest dinner concert ever!"

"I look forward to meeting more Candy Fairies," Mama G replied. She touched her stained dress. "But I am not sure what I will wear."

Berry flew over to her. "Oh, don't worry about that!" she said, winking at Melli and Raina. She looked over at Taly. "You too!"

"Thank you," Mama G said.

"Berry is the best," Melli said. "She will have you both styling for a castle dinner in no time."

Dash grinned. "This is going to be *so mint*!"

"Come with me," Berry said. Mama G and Taly followed her out.

Melli and the others weren't sure what to expect, but in a few moments Berry reappeared.

"Dash and some of the gnomes fixed the broken cart while we whipped up two dresses,"

Berry said. She looked around to make sure she had everyone's attention. "I'd like to present Mama G and Taly," the very proud Fruit Fairy announced.

Melli couldn't believe her eyes when the two dressed-up gnomes appeared. Berry had created two beautiful dresses trimmed with rock candy crystals.

"Oh, Berry!" Melli cried. "These dresses are beautiful! You both look delicious!"

Mama G looked embarrassed by all the attention, but Taly twirled around in her fancy swing skirt.

"We'd better get going if we are going to get to the castle," Melli said.

"Follow me," Mama G said to the Candy Fairies. "There is an old mining shortcut out

to Sugar Valley. And I believe there is an open-ing by the Royal Gardens."

"Sweet sugars!" Raina said. "I can't wait to record this in the Fairy Code Book!"

"This is sure to be a night to remember," Dash added. "And since the carts are fixed, we can take a ride to the tunnel opening!"

Mama G liked that idea. She sat up in the front of the cart with Dash to show her the old tracks that led out to the Royal Gardens. She looked over at Taly. "This is a big honor!"

"Thank you," Taly said to Melli, who was sitting beside her.

Melli was so excited to present her new friends to the kingdom. She no longer felt nervous. She was happy and eager to share her news of new friends with Princess Lolli and Prince Scoop and to share the treasures of Rock Candy Caves.

"This is it," Mama G called out. "We need to move these stones to find the exit."

The Candy Fairies, Mama G, and Taly lined up and removed the stones. Just as Mama G had said, the opening of the tunnel was a short distance from the entrance to the Royal Gardens.

"I must have passed these rocks a million times," Melli said, looking back at the opening.

"I never thought that this could be a tunnel down along Chocolate River and behind the falls."

"There are secrets all over Sugar Valley," Raina said.

"And supernice friends," Taly added, grinning happily. She spun around. "That is the most *rock-tacular* castle I have ever seen!"

"What until you see inside," Berry told her.

Melli took Taly's hand and Mama G's hand. "Come," she said. "It's time you met Princess Lolli and Prince Scoop."

CHAPTER 10

Happy Surprise

Two Royal Fairy Guards were standing at the gates of Candy Castle and gave Melli a strange look as she approached. A few bright stars shone in the night sky, and the moon was full. There were many Candy Fairies from Candy Kingdom, Sugar Kingdom, and Cake Kingdom, all ready to celebrate with Princess

Lolli and Prince Scoop. Melli took a deep breath. She tried to gather all the courage she could and gave Taly's and Mama G's hands a tight squeeze. As nervous as she was, she was sure the gnomes were feeling even more nervous about walking into a Candy Fairy castle.

"Rock-solid castle," Taly whispered. "I never imagined this place was so beautiful and delicious."

Melli smiled, then walked up to one of the guards. "We are here for the royal banquet," she said, "and we have brought two very special guests."

"Do Princess Lolli and Prince Scoop know?" the guard asked. He checked the scroll in his hand. "Are these guests on the list?"

"I am Melli the Caramel Fairy and these

are my guests," Melli said. "We'd like permission to see the princess. We're sure Princess Lolli would want to meet our new friends." She smiled at Mama G and Taly.

"Please let us have a moment with the princess," Raina added. "She's really going to want to meet our guests."

The guard looked over the Candy Fairies and the two gnomes. This was not the usual type of group to appear at the castle gates. He motioned for them to step to the side and spoke in hushed tones to the other guard.

"Don't worry," Melli told Mama G and Taly. "These guards can be a little sour sometimes."

"Maybe this wasn't such a great idea," Mama G said. She pulled at her dress. Melli thought she was feeling uncomfortable out of the caves and in the new fancy outfit that Berry had made.

Just then the guard came back over and told them to follow him. Inside the castle Melli felt lots of eyes on them as they walked to the throne room. No one said a word. She knew in her heart that once they met with Princess Lolli, all would be right.

The guard knocked on the door, then walked inside. "May I present Melli the Caramel Fairy and some friends," he said.

Princess Lolli came over to the door. She smiled at Mama G and Taly. "Sweet sugar-plums," she said, placing her hand on her chest. "Please come in," she added, seeing the worried looks on the gnomes' faces. "I am surprised to see you, but it is a very happy surprise. Welcome to Candy Castle!"

Prince Scoop flew over. "It is my great pleasure to meet you," he said. He swept his hand down to his waist as he gave a royal bow.

Mama G nearly fainted. "Oh, you are so kind," she said. "The pleasure is ours."

"You are so pretty!" Taly exclaimed, looking up at Princess Lolli.

Princess Lolli knelt down. "Thank you," she said. "And so are you! What is your name?"

"I am Crystal, but my friends call me Taly," she told the princess. "Please call me Taly."

Melli stepped forward. "I found Taly in Caramel Hills," she explained. "She was looking for supplies to fix their sugar carts and got lost. And this is Mama G," she said. "My friends and I brought Taly back to her home in the caves behind Chocolate Falls."

"Caves at Chocolate Falls?" Prince Scoop perked up.

"So it is true that there are caves behind the falls?" Princess Lolli said.

"We try to stay hidden," Mama G said. "We never wanted to bother the Candy Fairies."

"It is no bother," Princess Lolli said. "We are so pleased to know that you are here in Sugar Valley. Prince Scoop and I were talking about fairy tales we heard when we were young about gnomes and sugar crystals."

Taly stepped forward. "We have a crystal for you and Prince Scoop." She handed Princess Lolli a box.

The princess smiled. "This is such a treat,"

she said. "You'll sit at our table for the meal as our honored guests."

"And for the music!" Taly perked up. "Melli is really talented!"

Melli smiled. She felt so happy that the gnomes were there with her at the castle.

"Let's go to the ballroom," Prince Scoop said.

Mama G looked very nervous. "Are you sure? I know we are a bit of a shock."

"Oh, sugar sticks," Princess Lolli replied. "You are our guests!"

The princess and prince led the way to the grand ballroom. Again, Melli felt all eyes on them. But this time she realized that all the fairies in the room looked happily surprised. A round of applause sounded as they entered.

"Please welcome our friends from Rock

Candy Caves," Princess Lolli said. She bowed to the guests and everyone cheered. "Many of you may not know about the secret gnomes of Rock Candy Caves. Prince Scoop and I thought the gnomes were tales spun by fairies long ago." She stopped and pointed to Melli. "But Melli's kindness to the gnomes led her to a great discovery and new friends for us all."

Melli thought she would burst with pride. She quickly took her place on the stage with her licorice stick. "I'd like to dedicate this song to Taly and Mama G," she said. She raised her licorice stick to her lips and began to play. At the end of the song, she heard loud cheers, and Taly came running up to her.

"You played every note perfectly!" Taly exclaimed.

Melli blushed. "Thank you, Taly. You listened to me practice, so you really know the song well."

The meal was served, and Taly was extremely

well behaved. Melli saw that she was trying extra hard to be polite and well mannered. Mama G was beaming with pride.

At the end of the dinner, Taly's lip began to quiver. "I don't want to say goodbye," she said.

"It's not good-bye for long," Melli told her. "We're friends now, and we can visit each other." She looked over at Mama G. "That is, when you have permission to come visit me."

Mama G cuddled Taly. "I think Taly is going to have many visits to Caramel Hills in her future," she said.

"Sure as sugar," Taly said, smiling at the Candy Fairies. She took a purple-and-pink sugar crystal from her pocket and handed it to Melli. "Please keep this to remember me."

"I won't forget you," Melli said. "But I will

treasure this treat." She folded the crystal in her hand. "Thank you, Taly."

"Here's to Mama G and Taly!" Prince Scoop cheered.

"With many thanks to Melli and the Candy Fairies!" Mama G exclaimed.

Everyone applauded and continued to enjoy a royally good time together at Candy Castle.

Sparkle Spa

Making friends one Sparkly nail at a time!

EBOOK EDITIONS ALSO AVAILABLE

From Aladdin • KIDS.SimonandSchuster.com

Goddess Girls

READ ABOUT ALL
YOUR FAVORITE GODDESSES!

**#17 AMPHITRITE
THE BUBBLY**

**#16 MEDUSA
THE RICH**

**#15 APHRODITE
THE FAIR**

**#14 IRIS
THE COLORFUL**

**#13 ATHENA
THE PROUD**

**#12 CASSANDRA
THE LUCKY**

**#11 PERSEPHONE
THE DARING**

**#10 PHEME
THE GOSSIP**

**#1 ATHENA
THE BRAIN**

**#2 PERSEPHONE
THE PHONY**

**#3 APHRODITE
THE BEAUTY**

**#4 ARTEMIS
THE BRAVE**

**#5 ATHENA
THE WISE**

**#6 APHRODITE
THE DIVA**

**#7 ARTEMIS
THE LOYAL**

**THE GIRL GAMES:
SUPER SPECIAL**

**#8 MEDUSA
THE MEAN**

**#9 PANDORA
THE CURIOUS**

EBOOK EDITIONS ALSO AVAILABLE
From Aladdin
KIDS.SimonandSchuster.com

Did you LOVE reading this book?

Visit the Whyville...

IN THE MIDDLE BOOK HIVE

Where you can:

- ◯ Discover great books!
- ◯ Meet new friends!
- ◯ Read exclusive sneak peeks and more!

Log on to visit now!
bookhive.whyville.net